D0479244

HALLOWEEN

Scary Halloween Stories

Arnie Lightning

Arnie Lightning Books

Copyright © 2016 by Hey Sup Bye Publishing

All rights reserved. This book is a work of fiction. Graphics used in this book are licensed and © Dollar Photo Club. No part of this book or this book as a whole may be used, reproduced, or transmitted in any form or means without written permission from the publisher.

ISBN-13: 978-1535380737
ISBN-10: 153538073X

*"Be careful what you wish for...
It might just come true!"*

–Unknown

CONTENTS

FREE GIFT

"It's Okay to Be Different" is a beautifully illustrated story about accepting and celebrating others for their differences. It's a great way to teach children to appreciate and accept others for who they are.

To claim your FREE GIFT, simply go to www.ArnieLightning.com/freegift and enter your email address. Shortly thereafter, I will send you a free eBook for you to enjoy!

Please visit: www.ArnieLightning.com/freegift

Night Landscape

Roger drove slowly down the country road. It was midnight, and with not a streetlight in sight, he could only barely make out the road ahead of him. The pavement seemed to materialize in the beams of the car's headlights, disappearing just the same in the red glow by the rear of the car. To either side of him lay dark, featureless countryside. He would glance out the side windows from time to time, hoping to see some kind of light, some sign of people, but for the last hour there had been nothing.

His phone died two hours ago, and with it he had lost his only guidance. From then on he depended on his own sense of direction and the few maps he had stuffed in his glove compartment. Neither had been of any help to him. He did not know this area at all. Even if it were light out he would be lost, but with even the light of the moon hidden behind clouds he was completely hopeless. He did not even know how long he had been on this road, but it felt like ages since he had seen an intersection or even a sign.

Roger checked his rear-view mirrors. Maybe he would see the twin lights of another car. At least then he would not be alone. He may even let them pass him so he could follow them out of here. There was nothing but an infinite void behind him. He shuddered and looked at the right side mirror. At least through that he could see the landscape. At least through that he could see the end of the darkness as the land gave way to the dark blue sky.

A mountain in the distance behind him caught his eye. It was just like the land around it, a constant black shape that cut upwards into the sky, but something about it upset him to his core. It sent a chill about his whole body. He had spent too much time looking back, he turned his gaze back to the road ahead of him.

The road curved and twisted. As he drove up subtle hills the shadows that lay just beyond his headlights seemed to rise up from the ground. He shook his head. It was nonsense. A trick of the light. As he reached the top of these hills the shadows proved to be just that, flat sections of darkness that soon disappeared as the light pushed through them. He laughed quietly. He needed to find somewhere to stop and sleep.

The laughter died in his throat as he looked back at his right side mirror. He realized just what it was about the mountain that had upset him. When he had looked back before there was no mountain. And as he looked back at the passing landscape the mountain was again gone. He pressed on the accelerator and gripped the wheel tightly. He could not stop here!

The Phone

It was such an odd thing. At least, to me it seemed odd. I could not think of any reason to have a telephone in a graveyard, but I will admit that there is a possible use for one. I did not even think it would work. It hung against a tree at an odd angle, no visible wires connecting it to the phone lines that ran from pole to pole at the graveyard's border.

Curious, I picked the receiver up and held it to my ear. Sure enough, a dial tone hummed. I played with the dial, dragging it around in a circle so I could hear it whir back into place. I tapped the button in the cradle to hang up and then started to dial my home. I wanted to be sure this phone really worked. There was a ringing sound in the receiver. I held it away from my ear and listened carefully. My house was not far from where I stood. I listened, but could not make out any sound over the passing traffic.

The receiver started speaking. It was my mother. She asked who was calling. I giggled and hung up the phone. It really did work. Though that did not explain why it was there. A working phone out here in the graveyard? I shrugged and headed home.

That night, my parents left for a party, trusting me to take care of myself. I took this opportunity to eat junk food and watch the movie channels late into the night, drifting to sleep on the couch. The phone woke me up harshly. I turned and fell onto the floor, scrambling to the telephone. I answered the phone. The other end of the line was silent save for the sound of someone breathing. A prank phone call I figured.

I told the other end that this was not going to scare me and that they should not bother calling again. It was not going to scare me and it would only be a waste of both our times. I hung up. Then I thought for a moment. There was a chance they would still call back, if I really wanted them to stop I would have to play by their rules. I dialed the star and then six and nine. A robotic voice read off the number that the pranksters had called from. I hung up and dialed the number.

A cool breeze blew in through an open window. The leaves outside rustled, the only noise that evening. As the phone rang the breeze slowed and then finally stopped. The world outside was totally silent. Except for one thing. A ringing noise. Somewhere out in the graveyard. It stopped on the third ring. I hung up before they could answer.

The House Party

Everyone knew about the house up on the hill. Everyone knew its history and its owner. Everyone knew about the parties that used to go on up there, the noise and lights that used to fill the house every weekend. Everyone knew about the last party. The night the house grew silent and stayed that way. The day after the party the police searched the house and found it empty.

Everyone knew these things, but no one knew why the parties continued every weekend since. No one understood where the lights were coming from. The electric company had shut the power off after the owner disappeared and stopped paying the bills, but each weekend the lights came on nonetheless. No one could explain the sounds that came from the house. From afar, it sounded like any other party that had gone on there. As one drew closer, the sounds changed. The happy cheers, the music, it all seemed to slow down, to meld into one single continuous noise.

Many had ventured up to the house to see what was happening. It became a local challenge to get as close as possible to the house before losing courage. Children went in groups, watching each other's efforts from the gate and cheering. Most turned around halfway up the hill as the light and sound grew too harsh. A few had made it as far as the front steps. Only two had made it to the door.

The twins, Marcus and Luke, had gone together. They held tightly to each other as the lights in the house started to hurt their eyes and the sounds of the party warped into a loud many voiced scream. They touched the doorknob together and opened the door. The children at the gate lost sight of the twins and called out to them. A few minutes later Luke came running back down the hill.

The next day, a search of the house found no trace of Marcus. The children of the town were forbidden to play their game. They did not need to be told twice. Luke especially did not want to go back to the house. He did whatever he could to avoid walking anywhere near it.

A few weeks later, Luke vanished too. Everyone said he ran away from town to get away from the house that took his brother. Everyone was sure of it. No one had noticed the invitation on Luke's desk to a party at the house on the hill, signed by Marcus.

Under the Bed

Christie lay in bed, staring at the ceiling. She was almost certain she had heard something, but she had been drifting asleep and it was so faint. She listened but there was no sound. She sighed and turned onto her side. Then she heard it again. A soft moaning. It was brief, but this time she was sure of what she heard. She sat up and scanned her room, listening for the sound.

"Hello?" she asked her dark room.

She was answered by another moan. Her back stiffened as she peered over the edge of her bed. The sound was coming from beneath her. Slowly, cautiously, Christie lowered herself down to look under her bed. What she saw made no sense. Though her head was upside down, she was looking at a right-side up bedroom, one not unlike her own. She stuck her hand in and touched the floor that should have been the underside of her bed. It was a solid floor with rough carpeting.

Leaning further under the bed, she could feel gravity pulling her toward the floor. She tumbled over and popped out into the different bedroom. She sat up and looked around. The moan rose up again, this time from right behind her. She turned around and saw, sitting on a bed not unlike her own, was a girl not unlike herself. Except, this girl's skin was gray and pulled too tight. Her mouth was too large and filled with sharp teeth at odd angles. The gray girl moaned again, pointing right at Christie.

Christie could not scream. Her entire body was frozen. Even the air in her lungs refused to move.

"Dad!" yelled the gray girl.

The gray girl continued to scream as Christie scrambled under the bed and came back out into her own room. She sat silently and stared at her bed, breathing heavily. She waited for the monster to come crawling after her, but after a while she realized it was not coming. Christie sighed, thank goodness whatever that thing was seemed just as scared of her as she was of it. She stood and went back to bed.

As she lay in bed, Christie heard a door open. A light clicked on underneath her bed.

She could hear a deep, growling voice say, "What's wrong, honey?"

The gray girl shrieked, "There's something under my bed!"

"Well," said the deep voice, "I guess I should have a look under there."

The Thing in My Dreams

I sat at the edge of my bed, rubbing sleep from my eyes. Sunlight sneaked its way through a gap in my curtains and landed right on my face. I recoiled away from the warm light and stood up. It had been a restless night. I had grown used to them.

Every night for the last three months had been spent in the same nightmare. Something with too many teeth chasing me through the neighborhood. Each night I tried changing my escape route but each night it still caught me. I would wake in the middle of the night in a cold sweat. When I finally found myself asleep again the creature would be waiting and the chase would start again.

The dream was always so vivid. It was too real. I would find myself walking past the same places I had run past in my dream and my body would go numb. Sometimes I would catch myself taking the same routes that I had tried in my dream. I would go out of my way to avoid entire blocks of the neighborhood.

I did not know what this creature was or why it chased me in my dreams. Some nights I would try to reason with it, others I would try to fight it off. None of it worked. The creature would not or could not speak, and it tore through my defenses like paper. All I could do was run, so every night, that is what I would do.

But standing in my room this particular morning, I thought back to that night's dream. Once again I had been cornered by the creature. It stalked forward, opening its wide mouth filled with rows upon rows of sharp teeth. Just it was about to close its jaws on me it stopped and pulled back. The creature was whimpering. I stared at the creature. It was afraid. I laughed and taunted the creature.

Then I heard something. A low rumbling noise that shook my entire body. The sound was coming from directly behind me. The creature turned and fled from the thing that made the noise. I turned to face it. I cannot remember what I saw, but when I saw it I woke up in a cold sweat.

Behind You

Something was following James. It had been following him all day. He could hear its footsteps in between his own. Everywhere he went it was not far behind. In the morning it had been a few yards away. By lunch it was never more than a few feet away. Now, as the sun began to set, it was so close he could feel its breath on his neck.

Whatever it was, it was always behind him. No matter how quickly he turned around or how confined a space he was in it was directly behind him. Around lunch he turned his back to the wall of a four story building, but when he walked forward he still heard the thing's footsteps following from behind. He could not see it in reflections or in the pictures he tried to take with his camera.

At first it had been annoying. It felt like a joke someone was playing on him, but now James felt threatened by whatever this was. Its footsteps perfectly matched his own, for a few moments he thought that it had left him but when he listened closely he could make out the difference between his steps and those of the thing. They fell just a bit harder than his own. Even the breathing, that was constantly warming the back of his neck, had started to fall in rhythm with his own. When he reached for things he could feel a presence, as if something were resting just against the back of his hand.

James sat in his living room with all the lights on. He sat and watched the clock and listened to the sounds of the thing that seemed to be just behind him in his chair. As the clock ticked forward he could feel the thing pulling closer. It was right up against him now. James shut his eyes and tried to block out the sound of its breathing. Then, suddenly it stopped.

James opened his eyes. He looked at the clock. It was midnight. Perhaps the thing had passed. Like a trial. James had overcome it. James let out a sigh in relief and felt it. The thing's breath. It breathed out through his own mouth with him. James tried to move but he felt locked in place. He struggled and sweated but his body refused to move. James' vision started to fade and he felt weak. As he started to lose consciousness he could feel himself stand up.

He heard his own voice say, "My turn."

And then everything went dark.

The Man in the Dark Blue Suit

Allison slammed the front door behind her and turned every lock. She peered through the door's peephole and saw him. A tall, thin man in a dark blue suit. She had seen him all day and thought it a coincidence. She saw men in suits around her most days, but when he was on the train with her and then in the parking lot ahead of her she realized something was wrong. That was when she finally got a good look at his face. It was always smiling. The eyes were too big and had no color. The hair seemed fake, almost like a solid mass of plastic.

He was on the corner when she turned her car into the driveway and now he was right outside her door. Allison reached for the phone. There was no signal. Same went for her cellphone. She flicked a light switch and nothing happened. All of this had to happen now. She had lost cellphone service and suffered black-outs before, but why did they have to all happen at once now that she really needed these things.

There was a knock on the door. A slow, steady knock. One beat every five seconds. She did not have to check the peephole to know who it was. She did not want to check. She knew that when she did she would just see that awful face right in front of her. The knocking continued at the same pace, but each knock grew louder. She could hear the door straining against each blow. Was he trying to knock the door down?

As if to answer, the next knock sent a few fragments of wood scattering onto the floor. Allison ran to the back of the house. She weighed her options. She could not stay here, not when that thing was going to break in eventually, but the fence in her backyard was too high. She would have to run past her front door to escape. Could she get to her car before it noticed her? What would it do if it did? She decided to wait. If she left as the thing entered her house she could run around the outside of the house while it searched the inside.

Allison listened. Even from back here she could hear the sounds of her door being smashed open. She opened her back door and ran straight into the man in the dark blue suit.

"Going somewhere?" he asked.

She turned to run but he was behind her too. She looked out of her window and saw dozens more standing outside.

"Come with us, if you please," they spoke in unison.

Do Not Look

You have heard them before. Just as you are falling asleep and your mind and body start to numb. Something scratching at the window, or breaking the branches off trees, or scrambling across your roof. You hear these things and, as you just want to sleep, say this is just the wind. But you know this is not true. In the back of your mind, the part that is still active as the rest of it falls asleep, you know that these are the sounds belong to the things that live in the night.

You have seen them too. That quick, fleeting shadow that jumps through the light cast through your window. Those shaking trees on calm, breezeless nights. Even in the day you may have seen them in the corner of your eye. You may have caught them knocking something over on their way back into the shadows before you get a proper look at them.

You have seen and heard them, and even when you explain to yourself that these are just regular noises or tricks of the light you know the truth. You know the truth and it scares you. But you hide behind your lie to stay calm, to feel safe. Little do you know is that this ignorance, however false, is actually making you safe.

They hate being seen and heard. They belong to the shadows and to be known hurts them as much as the all-revealing sun. It burns them to be noticed. And when they burn they lash out to try and stop the pain. They retreat from your accidental glances, but if you were to look directly at them they would scream. A scream so loud and piercing you would think it were your own if not for the unnatural tones it produced. This scream would drown out everything, even your cries for help as they attacked.

So go to bed as soon as you can. Shut your windows and keep them locked. Close the curtains and shut off the lights. Close your eyes, cover your ears and go to sleep as fast as you can. And if you hear a tapping at the window, do not look. Something forces its way in and drops to the floor. Do not look. It crawls along the floor. Do not look. It climbs onto the foot of your bed. Do not look. If you value your life, no matter what, do not look!

Don't Believe in Ghosts

"I don't believe in ghosts," said Mary.

Dave had spent the past ten minutes on their way home from school telling her about the haunted house in town he had just heard about. Dave was new in town, so everyone took great pleasure in telling him about the house. Mary had heard the stories before and found them all quite boring. This is why, as much as she enjoyed Dave's company, she made no effort not to crush Dave's enthusiasm when he related these stories back to her.

"Not even a little bit?" asked Dave.

"No, Dave, not even a little bit. Everyone makes it all up just because the house looks a little different than the rest."

"What does it look like?" Dave asked, still eager to learn more about this local oddity.

"Just like any other house," Mary said, "It's just a little older than the rest. It's been around for a long time."

"How long?"

"How should I know?"

Dave stopped and stared across the street. They were standing in front of the house he had heard about so much in school. It was covered by faded blue paint and large, dusty windows. The steeply sloped roof rose up in two points at the top of two circular outcroppings. Surrounding the house was an iron fence topped with menacing barbs. Mary snapped her fingers in front of Dave's dumbfounded face.

"Dave! It's just a house."

"How are you so sure?"

"Because there's no such thing as ghosts. Have you ever seen a ghost?"

Dave shuffled his feet. "No, but I haven't seen the wind either."

Mary rolled her eyes. "That's a poor analogy. Look, I'll prove it to you that it's just a house."

Mary turned and crossed the street. Dave, not wanting her to go but too scared to move any closer to the house, reached out to her.

"Hey, wait!" Dave called after Mary.

Mary ignored Dave and boldly walked up to the old house. She opened the door and disappeared inside.

"Hey Mom, I'm home!" Mary called out. "I'm going over to a friend's house!"

"Just be back before dark," Mary's mother called back from somewhere in the house.

Mary left the house and rejoined Dave, who was awestruck at her supposed bravery. After that he stopped listening to the stories and stopped believing in ghosts. Dave and Mary became good friends they were practically inseparable. The rest of the kids at school wondered why Dave spent all of his time alone.

A Familiar House

I could not remember why I was here. The door slammed shut behind me. I looked around. It was dark, but a faint blue light filtered through the curtained windows, illuminating the room. It looked familiar, like I had been here before, but I knew this was not my house. So why was I here?

I was in a living room. A sagging couch sat in front of an old television. On the wall were some photos, but in the dim light I could only make out basic shapes. A clock ticked loudly on the wall ahead of me. I walked over to the television and held my hand against it. No static, did it even work? I tried the dial on its face and nothing happened. The light switch on the wall did nothing as well.

I moved into the adjacent kitchen. A pot of stale water sat on a cold stove. The refrigerator was empty and filled with lukewarm air. On the table in the center of the room sat a bowl of plastic fruit. I tried to open the oven but it would not budge. Nothing for me here I returned to the living room. There was nowhere else to go but up the stairs.

I walked up three steps and hit my head against a wall. The stairs stopped a short way up and the rest of it was a painted surface. There was no second floor. Where was I? Why was I here? I looked around more frantically. The blue light from the windows reflected off the glass of one of the photos hanging on the wall. I picked it up and held it closer to the light to get a better look. At first I thought it was a family photo. A group of people gathered closely together and looking straight at the camera. In the dim blue light I saw that the family had been blended together into a solid mass with five heads. Their faces had been smeared beyond recognition. This was not a real photo. None of them were.

I opened the curtain to see just where I was. Behind the curtain was a solid black wall and a blue-tinted flood light. I dropped the photo and ran for the door. Where was this place? How did I end up here? I had to find out. I wrenched the door open and ran through. I was back in the same living room. I could not remember why I was here. The door slammed shut behind me.

ABOUT THE AUTHOR

Arnie Lightning is a dreamer. He believes that everyone should dream big and not be afraid to take chances to make their dreams come true. Arnie enjoys writing, reading, doodling, and traveling. In his free time, he likes to play video games and run. Arnie lives in Mississippi where he graduated from The University of Southern Mississippi in Hattiesburg, MS.

For more books by Arnie Lightning please visit:
www.ArnieLightning.com/books

Made in the
USA
Columbia, SC

78686904R00022